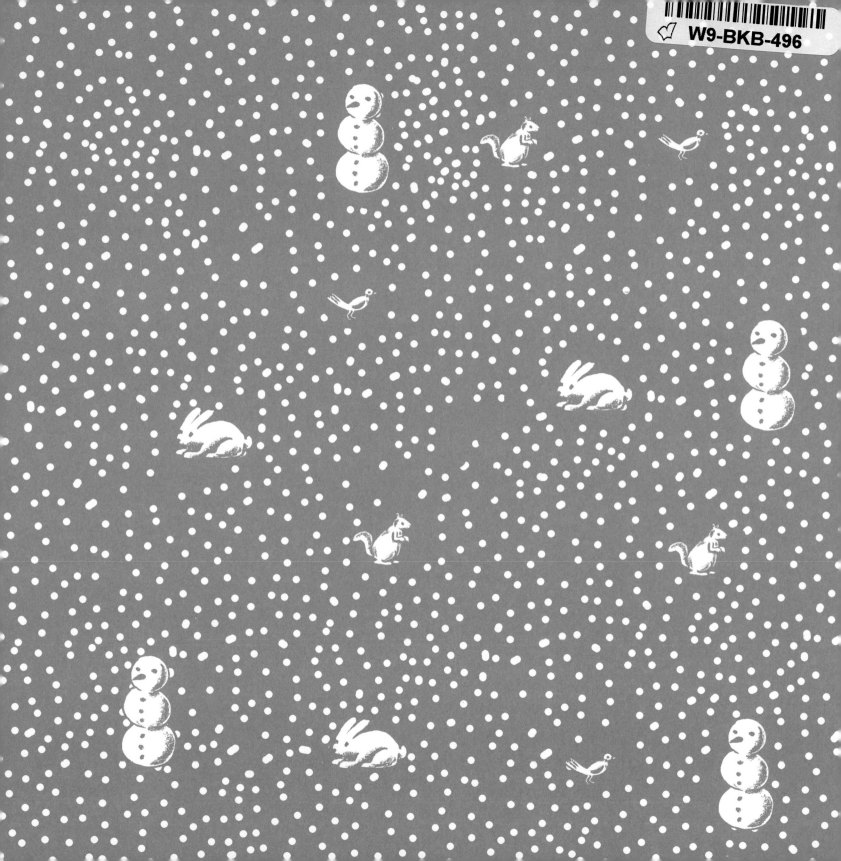

SMALL WALT

Story by **Elizabeth Verdick**

Pictures by **Marc Rosenthal**

A PAULA WISEMAN BOOK
Simon & Schuster Books for Young Readers
New York London Toronto Sydney New Delhi

SIMON & SCHUSTER BOOKS FOR YOUNG READERS
An imprint of Simon & Schuster Children's Publishing Division
1230 Avenue of the Americas, New York, New York 10020
Text copyright © 2017 by Elizabeth Verdick • Illustrations copyright © 2017 by Marc Rosenthal
SIMON & SCHUSTER BOOKS FOR YOUNG READERS is a trademark of Simon & Schuster, Inc.
For information about special discounts for bulk purchases, please contact
Simon & Schuster Special Sales at 1-866-506-1949 or business@simonandschuster.com.
The Simon & Schuster Speakers Bureau can bring authors to your live event.
For more information or to book an event, contact the Simon & Schuster Speakers Bureau
at 1-866-248-3049 or visit our website at www.simonspeakers.com.
Book design by Lizzy Bromley • The text for this book was set in Archetype.
The illustrations for this book were rendered in Prismacolor pencil and digital color.
0218 PCH
4 6 8 10 9 7 5 3
Library of Congress Cataloging-in-Publication Data
Verdick, Elizabeth. • Small Walt / Elizabeth Verdick ;
illustrated by Marc Rosenthal.—First edition. • pages cm
"A Paula Wiseman Book." • Summary: Small Walt is the smallest snowplow in the fleet
and he always gets picked last, but when there is a big snowstorm in the city,
he will have the chance to prove his worth.
ISBN 978-1-4814-4845-1 (hardcover)
ISBN 978-1-4814-4846-8 (eBook)
[1. Stories in rhyme. 2. Snowplows—Fiction. 3. Size—Fiction.]
I. Rosenthal, Marc, 1949– illustrator. II. • Title.
PZ8.3.V712639Sm 2017
[E]—dc23 • 2015000065

FOR DAN,
who always believes in me
—E. V.

FOR EILEEN,
who keeps me honest and makes me happy
—M. R.

BRRRR, the night air is cold and wet.
The city plows stand in a row, ready to fight the snow.

There's Walt, the smallest snowplow in the fleet.
Maybe this time he won't get picked last.

"I'm not taking the little guy!" says Big Buck.
"Neither am I," says Hank. "He's too small for a big snow like this."

Walt waits and waits . . .

and waits.

"*I'll* drive him," says Gus.

Gus starts Walt up.

He checks Walt's load
of ice-melting salt.

He inspects the salt spreader—
switch, *twist*.

He tests the plow—
up, down—

and the lights—
off, on.

"Good to go," says Gus.

The other drivers head out first,
plow after plow after plow.
Fat snowflakes hit the windshield—
splat-splat—while Walt waits his turn.
Big Buck *HONK HONK*s.
"Try to keep up, Small Stuff!" he shouts.
Grrrr, Walt's engine growls.

Each plow has a route to follow.
Walt knows where to go.

First the bridges—icy!

Then the ramps—dicey!

Walt's tires grip the road—*rumble-grumble*.
His lights flash—*wink, blink*.
His plow pushes the snow—*scraaaatch, scraaaape*—
and his spreader scatters salt—*swoosh-whoosh*.

His engine hums:
My name is Walt.
I plow and I salt.
I clear the snow
so the cars can go!

The radio squawks: "Citywide blizzard!
Head home, folks. Head home!"
But snow-fighters work all-nighters. . . .

Sleet pelts Walt's windows.
The wind whips his sides.
Long lanes loom ahead.

Walt plows on, mile after mile after mile.

So much slush and muck!

Don't get stuck. . . . Don't get stuck.

His engine thrums:
My name is Walt.
I plow and I salt.
They say I'm small,
but I'll show them all.

Whoa! There's a hill ahead—a high, high hill.
"I've never seen such big drifts.
I don't think we're up to this," says Gus.
Walt slows.

Behind Walt, two bright headlights blaze.
It's Big Buck.

"We could let Buck plow the hill," says Gus.
Walt's engine revs. *Errr Vroom-vaRoom!*
"Okay," says Gus. "I hear you."

So up they go . . . up . . .
uuuup . . . uh-oh!

Walt's back end skids,
slips down,
down . . .

He shudders, sputters. But . . .
*A plow and salter
can never falter.
Plow and salter,
never falter.*

"Want to try again, Walt?"
VROOM-VROOM—VROOOOOM!
Gus hits the gas.

Walt climbs up, *up*, UP to the very tip, *tip* TOP where . . .

he stops.

Oh, that's a *loooooong* way down.

"You can do it, Walt!"
Not too small, not too small.
His engine drums:
We're Gus and Walt.
We plow and we salt.
We'll fight the snow.
Get ready—now GO!

Together they forge a path
down that steep, steep hill,
leaving a trail of salt—
and Big Buck—behind them.

"We did it, Walt!" says Gus.
Errrrnnnntttt! HissssYesssssss.
Beep-beep!

At dawn—*YAWN*—Gus and Walt
head back to the lot.
Gus hollers hello.
Hank salutes.
And Big Buck says, "The little guy
did a better job than I thought."
ChuggaMmmm-hmmm!

Gus chuckles. Then he takes off his winter scarf
and ties it in a bow on Walt's rearview mirror.
"A blue ribbon for my buddy."
Walt's engine purrs.
Never faltered. . . . Never faltered.
Gus pats the dashboard and says good night.

The plows stand in a row, ready to fight the snow.
Small Walt is still the littlest in line,
but he's got a big blue ribbon . . .
and good old Gus.
"See you tonight, Snow-fighter!"

To:

From:

Thank You God, Good Night

Written by
Marianne Richmond

Illustrations by Dubravka Kolanovic

sourcebooks
jabberwocky

Copyright © 2021 by Marianne Richmond
Cover and internal design © 2021 by Sourcebooks
Illustrations by Dubravka Kolanovic

Sourcebooks and the colophon are registered trademarks of Sourcebooks.

Watercolor was used to prepare the full color art.

Published by Sourcebooks Jabberwocky, an imprint of Sourcebooks Kids
P.O. Box 4410, Naperville, Illinois 60567–4410
(630) 961-3900
sourcebookskids.com

Library of Congress Cataloging-in-Publication Data is on file with the publisher.

Source of Production: 1010 Printing International, Kwun Tong, Hong Kong, China
Date of Production: Novemer 2021
Run Number: 5024380

Printed and bound in China.
OGP 10 9 8 7 6 5 4

Dedicated to
God's children everywhere.
—MR

Comfy bed, I'm all tucked in.
Cozy covers, feet to chin.

Splashy clean.

Favorite song.

Snuggled up where I belong.

One more thing
before I dream...
Thank you, God,
for everything!

Thank you, God, for this day.

Each a blessing
sent my way.

Thank you, God,
for family dear.

Helpers, teachers, far and near.

Thank you, God,
for friends and fun.

Memory making,
rain or sun.

Thank you, God,
for where we live.
Enough to share
and help and give.

Thank you, God,
for flowers, trees.

Nature's beauty
we receive.

Thank you, God, for being you—
faithful, steady, good, and true.

Thank you, God, for your light.
Hope for those in need tonight.

Thank you, God, for your peace.
Any worry yours to keep.

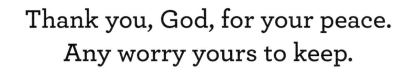

Thank you, God, for your love.
Inside my heart, around, above.

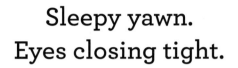

Sleepy yawn.
Eyes closing tight.

Thank you, God,
amen, good night.

MARIANNE RICHMOND is a bestselling author and artist who has touched the lives of millions for more than two decades by creating books that celebrate the love of family. Visit her at mariannerichmond.com.

"My books help you share your heart and connect with those you love."

DUBRAVKA KOLANOVIC studied at the Savannah College of Art and Design in Savannah, Georgia, and at the Academy of Fine Arts in Zagreb, Croatia, where she received her degree in painting. She published her first book in the United States at the age of eighteen. Since then, she has devoted herself to children's book illustration. Dubravka is very proud of her long-standing collaboration with UNICEF, for whom she has designed more than eighty cards and posters. She was also nominated for a Hans Christian Andersen Award in 2020. For several years, Dubravka has volunteered with environmental protection projects all over the world, from the Amazon rainforest to the Arctic. She lives and works in Zadar, a small town on the Mediterranean coast in Croatia with her husband; her children Marko, Ivan, and Dorcas; and their dog Kiki.